Expectation

A FRANCESCA FRUSCELLA MYSTERY

T0307130

JEFFREY DESHELL

Expectation

A FRANCESCA FRUSCELLA MYSTERY

FC2

TUSCALOOSA

Copyright © 2013 by Jeffrey DeShell
The University of Alabama Press
Tuscaloosa, Alabama 35487-0380
All rights reserved
Manufactured in the United States of America

FC2 is an imprint of The University of Alabama Press

Book Design: Illinois State University's English Department's
Publications Unit; Director: Tara Reeser; Assistant Director:
Steve Halle; Production Assistant: Brian Hedgepeth
Cover Design: Lou Robinson
Typeface: Garamond

∞

The paper on which this book is printed meets the minimum
requirements of American National Standard for Information
Sciences—Permanence of Paper for Printed Library Materials,
ANSI Z39.48–1984

Library of Congress Cataloging-in-Publication Data
DeShell, Jeffrey.
 Expectation : a Francesca Fruscella mystery / Jeffrey DeShell.
   pages cm
 ISBN 978-1-57366-175-1 (pbk. : alk. paper) — ISBN 978-1-
57366-843-9 (e-book)
 1. Women detectives—Fiction. 2. Murder—Investigation—
Fiction. I. Title.
 PS3554.E8358E94 2013
 813'.54—dc23
                                        2013013564

TO PATRICK GREANEY

Music is similar to language. Expressions like musical idiom or musical accent are not metaphors. But music is not language. Its similarity to language points to its innermost nature, but also toward something vague. The person who takes music literally as a language will be led astray by it.

—t. w. adorno, "music, language, and composition"

ACKNOWLEDGMENTS

I would like to thank Robert Steiner, Lynne Tillman, Marco Breuer and Ted Pelton for their help and support throughout. Special thanks go to Lisa Harrington, who explained a lot, and the students in my various graduate Modernism courses at the University of Colorado at Boulder. I am extremely grateful to all at FC2. I would also like to thank Elisabeth Sheffield, whom I love with all of my ragged heart.

Expectation

A FRANCESCA FRUSCELLA MYSTERY

CHAPTER 1

Fünf Klavierstücke
op. 23

I. sehr langsam

Investigation of murder involves the ability to recognize and articulate patterns: sometimes the patterns are spatial, evidence restricted to specific sites. Motifs of time require the detective to excavate and sift, fact often the wallflower, remains reluctant, outline blending into obscure background. Crimes of passion are the easiest to understand and solve: love, often wonderfully sweet, can leave horrific stains, blotting through white sheets, marks on paper indicting their author. After choking or stabbing, killers, now the aggrieved, are truculent, victims forced into self-protective acts. Patterns of psychopaths can frustrate the detective: in examining and comprehending deviance, often the investigator falters, comforting logic overwhelmed by true strangeness. Scenes of psycho-murder are the most difficult, with all gathering and analyzing futile initially, the design appearing only in repetition, vanishing until a subsequent recurrence.

The corpse is vital, a dominant component of the pattern. The body originates both the crime and the investigation: it's the key signature to the piece. Motive is secondary, only a lesser component. Like a Brahms melody created through the demands of harmony, the motive can actually distract from recognition, leading the investigator down cul-de-sacs, allowing the more productive trails to cool. The corpse here, indeed everything first noticed, seemed to fit seamlessly into the affair-gone-wrong husband-prime-suspect television stage set of the Oxford hotel room. The body, that of a tanned and toned woman in her wealthy thirties, was nude, tied spread eagle on the bed. A large plume of dried blood shocked the cream colored wall: both carotid arteries had likely been severed.

"Detective."

"Detective."

"What are you doing here?"

"I was in the neighborhood."

"This is my case."

"I know that. Don't get nervous."

"I'm not nervous. Stay out of my way."

"If you need any help…"

"I won't. Stay out of my way."

While he turned abruptly, almost tripping over a technician, I surreptitiously, without gloves, examined her clothes—a nice size four Armani jacket suit and matching skirt—that were carefully folded and hung over the chair. He was right, it wasn't my case, and I was in the way. But he'd never acted like that to me before.

I stepped closer. The flesh was firm: she pilatied and watched her diet. She undressed well, her skin was clear, limbs shaped and displayed for maximum effect. It hadn't been enough: her killer had been unimpressed. He'd done nothing but cut her throat. He'd killed dispassionately, the knife slicing clinically, tissue parting and opening without resistance. She stretched out elegantly, too pampered to be someone's woman kept. And didn't that pose, stiffening, indicate clearly that she was a willing participant, expecting not dreading her partner's return?

"Leave. Now."

"The dick returns, abrasive."

"I don't want or need your help."

CHAPTER 2

Vier Lieder
op. 2

I. Erwartung

I closed my office door and opened the window blinds, letting the late afternoon April sun stream through. The bright yellow light was stronger than I expected and I squinted, shielding my eyes with my hand. Looking down at the small entrance plaza, and then at the parking lot across the street, I thought about all the work I had: a likely gang drive-by and a relatively straightforward escalated barfight. The image of that woman at the Oxford—tanned limbs against the white of the sheets, the black blood dark against the cream colored wall—came to me and I began to feel sorry for her. I hadn't felt anything while I was there, save a mild interest in trying to uncover a pattern. But now, as I thought of her splayed open, well, I hoped they didn't find me like that. No matter who or what she was, that was no way to go out. And Benderson's behavior nagged.

I heard a knock and turned.

Captain Schlaf, a large, well-built man, walked into my office and closed the door. Besides his block-like shape, the captain had two defining characteristics: he looked like he needed to wear glasses, and he sported a huge green and red ring, big as a ping-pong ball, from his college football team. He was always working that fucking thing, twisting it, sliding it up and down his finger, moving his hand back and forth and admiring it from different focal distances.

"Fruscella, where are you in the Kinney case?"

"Confession imminent and, according to the DA, a likely plead to manslaughter."

"You going to send the drive-by to Gangs?"

"I want to check out a couple of things first."

He leaned forward and put his hands on the desk. His ring caught the light and sparkled: green, red, green, like a Christmas disco ball.

"You recognize the stiff at the Oxford?"

"No."

"Does the name Magdalena Lowenthal ring any bells?"

The Lowenthals were a name in Southern Colorado when I was growing up: this was big. "No."

"Wife of state senator Augie Lowenthal? Best friend of one Peter Coors? You have heard of Coors, right?"

"My best friend in high school was a Coors."

He stopped working his ring and looked me in the eye. "The woman you saw on the bed at the Oxford was Magdalena Mary Lowenthal. This has priority, so I might need to take some of your team. Thought I'd let you know."

He turned and walked out quickly. It wasn't every day that a state senator's wife got herself kilt. An ambitious state senator as well, a pro-life and anti-immigration rising star with a smooth, dulcet voice, sweetening and stoking the sour shrill message of Caucasian resentment. He had a few enemies, which meant there'd be a few suspects. And he himself would be prime. But it wasn't my case.

II. Schenk mir Deinen goldenen Kamm

On April 2nd, 2009 at 14:30, I, officer Benny Guiterrez, was dispatched to the Oxford Hotel, 1600 17th Street, Denver CO in response to the discovery of a body in a room of the hotel. When I arrived, I was met by a Mr. Henry Larsson, 3237 Umatilla Street, Denver DOB 6/26/65, the assistant manager of the hotel, and a Mr. James Harold, 572 Race Street, Arvada DOB 8/6/57 desk clerk. Mr. Larsson told me that at approximately 2:10 pm, a Ms. Dolores Raez, of 1830 Sacramento Street Apt 1279 B DOB 2/13/78 Permanent Residence # 2398BZ459GZX23, maid, opened the door to clean the room, 242, and found the body. Ms. Raez immediately ran down the stairs to inform Mr. Harold, who called 911. Mr. Harold then called Mr. Larsson, who went to inspect the room. Mr. Larsson entered the room to ascertain if the victim still exhibited vitals and seeing that the victim was deceased, he locked the door and returned to the desk. He took Ms. Raez downstairs to the employees' room to comfort her.

I went up to Room 242, accompanied by Mr. Larsson, who unlocked the door. I asked him if he knew the identity of the woman, and if he had seen or heard anything unusual. He responded that he had arrived on duty at six am and had not seen or heard anything unusual. I ascertained the victim was deceased, and as I did so, the paramedics arrived. I called the station for backup and informed the Crimes Against Persons unit. I was ordered to secure the site and wait for the detectives. Mr. Larsson then told me that the woman had registered under the name of Magdalena Dehmel of Colorado Springs, and that he had seen her at the hotel at least two other times. At 14:39, Detective Benderson and Sergeant Owen of the Homicide Division arrived, and I reported what Mr. Larsson told me. I relinquished the crime scene to Detective Benderson and Sergeant Owen at 14:56.

Detective Benderson and I arrived at the Oxford Hotel, 1600 17th Street, Denver, on April 2nd, 2009 at 2:40 pm. We met the desk clerk, Mr. James Harold, 52, of 572 Race Street, Arvada, who escorted us to room 242, where we met Officer Benjamin Guiterrez, the first officer on the scene, and two paramedics. Officer Guiterrez informed us that at 2:38 pm he determined the victim was deceased, and that he then secured the site. He also informed us that according to Mr. Larsson, 34, of 3237 Umatilla Street, the body was found at 2:10 by the housecleaner, Ms. Dolores Raez, 28, of 1830 Sacramento Street Apt 1279. Officer Guiterrez informed us that Mr. Larsson had tentatively identified the body as that of a Ms. Magdelena Dehmel of Colorado Springs. Officer Guiterrez informed us that he had not formally interviewed Mr. Larsson, Mr. Harold or Ms. Raez.

At 3:03 pm, Officer Gutierrez relinquished the crime scene to Detective Benderson. Detective Benderson called in for uniform backup, and told Guiterrez to close off the entire floor. Detective Benderson checked for vital signs, and finding none, released the paramedics at 3:07, and informed the coroner's office. The victim's hands and her feet were tied to the four corners of the bed frame with leather cords. A great deal of dark liquid had pooled around her neck and head, and this dark liquid was beginning to thicken. A large splatter of this dark liquid occurred on the wall to her right. No signs of struggle or forced entry were visible in the room, clothes were folded neatly on a chair, and the window was closed and locked from the inside, the window overlooking Wazee Street below. At 3:12, Detectve Benderson instructed me to obtain preliminary statements from Ms. Raez and Mr. Larsson see attachments 1 and 2. Ms. Raez's English is not good, so I interviewed her in Spanish: she corroborated Mr. Larsson's statement. I checked the hotel records with Mr. Harold's permission, and found that a Ms. Magdalena Dehmel of Colorado Springs was a guest of the hotel four previous times, on December 12th of 2007, January 16th of 2008, March 30th of 2008 and September 21st of 2008, in addition to the night in question. In all cases, the room was paid for with a Visa Black Card registered to Magdalena Dehmel, with the address as 275 North 17th Street, Denver. I returned to the room at 3:50 pm: three uniformed officers had now secured the hall and were beginning to attempt to interview the guests in an adjacent room. Dr. Nehdjaru, coroner and his assistant, as well as three members of the Crime Scene Investigation Unit were now present in the room. I informed Detective Benderson of the results of my preliminary interviews with Raez and Larsson, as well as my investigations into the victim's previous visits. Detective Benderson informed me that the initial coroner's findings indicated the time of death was approximated between 2:30 and 3:30 the morning of April 2nd, and the likely cause of death was two severed carotid arteries. There was no preliminary evidence of sexual activity. Detective Benderson also informed me that he had located the victim's purse, and that her driver's license indicated the name of the victim as Magdalena Dehmel, Date of Birth August 17, 1964, address 275 North 17th Street, Denver, and that various credit cards with the names Magdalena Dehmel, Magdalena Lowenthal and Magdalena Dehmel Lowenthal were found along with her driver's license and $235 in cash. 3:57 Detective Fruscella arrived and logged in. After speaking with Detective Benderson, Detective Fruscella logged out at 4:07. The coroner and his assistant wrapped the body in a body bag at 4:20 and transported it to the morgue. Detective Benderson released the site to Detective Snow of the Crime Scene Investigation Unit at 4:47 pm.

III. Erhebung

Patterns in homicide are always there, always present. Sometimes we have to dig deep, deep into the bass as it were, to understand the fundamental motifs and movement. Other times, themes might be inaudible because we are too close: we need to step away from the stage to be able to hear anything over the bass and drums. And sometimes designs aren't comprehensible through our consciousness. Sometimes, we have to rely on our subconscious, our intuition, our ambient listening. Information can take on many forms, and often the direct approach is the least effective.

To insist that there exist patterns in all homicides is not to say that such patterns are always or even frequently discernible. Often, through lack of information, surplus of information, inadequate methods of detection, sheer exhaustion, bumbling coworkers, political or other extraneous pressures—there are many factors, an almost infinite number of variants and accidentals—people do in fact get away with murder. In the US last year, about 32% of homicide cases went unsolved, one in three. In Denver, we're a little better: if you kill someone here you only have a one in four chance of not being caught.

The most interesting thing about homicide patterns to me is that I often begin to understand them only when I come into contact with something that at first seems totally extraneous to that pattern. Dissonance in fact proves the key. In other words, there's only *apparent* dissonance, *apparent* contradiction, *apparent* ambivalence: if the detective studies the data with enough skill and care, *all* information fits the pattern at some level, with the most significant details often being the elements that at first seem most superfluous. Accidents happen, surely, but accidents too are part of the plan. For me it's the vagrant chords that tell the story. And the lack of vagrant chords, well, that itself is unusual.

Ah fuck, what difference did it make to me? I had enough trouble with a drive-by where nobody saw nothing. But now I was going home to my son, and perhaps his granddaddy had made green chili—I could smell something good as I left this morning.

I got my keys out of my purse. "Francesca!"

I turned to face Benderson.

"Listen, I'm sorry about today in the hotel."

Just as he had never, ever, treated me like he did at the Oxford Hotel he had never, ever, apologized to me. And two wrongs never, ever, make a right.

IV. Waldsonne

There was something wrong here, the faintest intimation of a theme I didn't want to hear. Benderson and I had been friends for more than twenty years, and, near the beginning of those twenty years, right after the Academy, we'd been more than friends. This wasn't to suggest I thought I knew him, far from it: we'd gone our separate ways and lived our separate lives, sometimes meeting for a drink, but usually finding reasons not to invite or accept. It wasn't like the Benderson I knew, however, to mark his territory, to have a pissing fight at a murder scene. And I could not recall a single time he had apologized to anyone for anything.

Right on Pecos and a stoplight at 32nd. Almost home. I always liked April light in Colorado. Around this time, seven, seven-thirty, the gold and sometimes orange and purple sunset settled into soft silver. There was a clarity, a lucidity obscured by the bright, glaring sunlight of the day. And this was the time that I often went home to my son.

I pulled into the driveway and saw Nick's bike on the porch of the house entrance. The thick metal chain was wrapped tightly around the stem of the seat: he hadn't put it away and he hadn't locked it to anything. Boy was careless, forgetful, and sadly mistaken if he thought I'd replace a stolen bicycle. And I loved him with all of the heart I had left.

The shop lights were still on, so I thought I'd stick my head in to say a few words to Hector, Nicholas' paternal grandfather. I could hear Wes Montgomery just before I opened the door. Hector was hunched over something back at his bench, the work light on and his soldering glasses covering his eyes. I noticed the acidic metal smell of the solder, and the bebop was coming from the right, maybe Studio D. I walked past the front counter and into Hector's inner sanctum. He flipped his lenses up and looked at me.

"I didn't hear you come in."

"Obviously. You lock the register?"

He nodded. "Got some good news: I sold a pair of the Cremonas to some guy from Vail. Trying to get him to take the Conrad Johnson monoblocks, but he likes McIntosh." He looked me up and down and said, "Maybe you could work on him?"

"I'm forty-seven, he must be eighty and you must be kidding. We should go celebrate the Cremonas."

"I already made chili."

"I saw Nick's bike."

"He was practicing until a minute ago."

"I'll see you up there. And don't work too long, I'm hungry."

I walked through the workshop and through the back door, then up the dark stairs, where the smell of hot wire and electrical heat was replaced by pork and green Pueblo chilies. As I opened the kitchen door, the spicy smell became palpable, and I could see Nicholas lounging on the living room couch, staring at something in his hand, probably his cellphone. I looked at his furrowed brow and smiled: he was easily the best thing that had ever happened to me.

"Hey, what are you doing?"

He didn't look up. "Texting."

"You need to lock your bike or put it in the garage."

"I will."

"You practice the Bach today?"

"Yeah."

CHAPTER 3

Fünf Klavierstücke
op. 23

II. sehr rasch

The body and surrounding site arranged to indicate suicide. Pistol gripped then mouthed, brains splattered now coagulating. Perfect. Just perfect. No sign of exterior struggle. No sign of other violence. The note on conspicuous laptop paraded as corroborating evidence.

The shed immaculate, except for corpse slumped and akimbo. And the blood, brains and late August flies. I, over ruined body bent, suspicions and nagging doubts growing. Sixto Gonsalvo, the driver's license confirmed, indicating the anomalous form beginning to smell. Sixto, the former pusher become gardener, dead, the former felon now nothing. Dead Sixto found in the gardening shed of Mr. August Lowenthal. Too much here.

"Where's the note on the computer?"

"Here Ma'am."

"Was the computer secured?"

"Both body and computer were found by a truck driver delivering gravel. He said he didn't bother anything, and when I arrived I secured the site as well as the computer."

My exhaustion and deep sadness say to kill myself. May God and my family forgive, for I love them. My experience and deep skepticism said this is all bullshit. No way suicide.

CHAPTER 4

Verklärte Nacht
op. 4

Interview Room A was new, like all of the rooms, but unlike all the rooms smelled more than faintly of piss. The walls were off-white, the table dark brown, and the hard chairs rigid plastic grey. A large, two-way mirror dominated the back wall.

"Mr. Bratsche, you were a good friend of Mr. Gonsalvo, were you not?"

"What am I doing here? Sixto killed himself."

"We haven't yet clarified the circumstances surrounding his death: please answer the question."

He snorted, "Circumstances surrounding his death? He bit the wrong end of a pistol's what I heard. Fuck lady, excuse my French: Sixto killed himself."

I stood up quickly and turned to the Sergeant. "I'm going to my office to give Mr. Felix Padilla, Mr. Bratsche's parole officer, a telephone call. I'd very much like Mr. Padilla to know how uncooperative Mr. Bratsche is being to our investigation, and how his refusal to answer questions in a timely manner, not to mention this vulgar, moronic and insulting persona he's for some reason adopting, is severely handicapping the efficacy of our inquiries. I will then thank Mr. Padilla for his recommendation of the reexamination of Mr. Bratsche's parole status."

"What do you want to know, Ma'am?"

"Detective. My name's Detective."

Sixto had a wife, and this wife lived in a sad little row house in east Aurora. I sat on a new couch in a narrow spotless living room, with competing television programs blaring through the walls on either side.

"I want you to find the man that killed my husband, detective."

"I don't understand. Sixto killed himself."

"We both know that ain't true."

"We haven't yet clarified the circumstances surrounding his death. Why do you think someone killed him?"

"I don't think, I know. I got my reasons, you know what I'm saying? One, Sixto ain't the type to kill himself. He was in Cañon, Max, for four years, and he didn't get down on hisself: he was always saying, 'I got some life to live, I got some things to see, some things to see,' you know what I'm saying?"

"So he never gave you any indication that suicide might be a viable solution to his problems?"

She shook her head, "What I just say?" She paused, both televisions also silent. "Man loved his grass, know what I'm saying?"

"I don't understand."

I caught up with Benderson in the hallway near the vending machines. He looked terrible: tired, pasty and gaunt.

"Got a minute?"

He looked at his wrist. "A minute."

"How's the Dehmel case?"

He shrugged and shook his head.

"Another JonBenet, huh?"

"Thirty seconds."

I tried my best shy smile, but it likely came off crooked. "You know Sixto Gonsalvo, Lowenthal's gardener?"

"Sixto killed himself."

"I don't think so, and that case is possibly related to your case. So I'll need your notes, and files, docs, anything you can give me, by tomorrow."

"I don't understand: like I said, Sixto killed himself."

"We both know that's not true."

He shrugged, "Tomorrow, then."

We met Mr. Curtis Samuels, Sixto's supervisor, underneath a large oak tree at the edge of a football field-sized green lawn. He was much younger than I expected, and in his basketball shorts, flip-flops, baseball cap and very dark sunglasses, he looked like an advertisement for big-boned stupidity.

"Thank you for meeting us, Mr. Samuels."

"Mr. Lowenthal told us all to give you any help you needed. Though I don't know why: everyone knows Sixto capped himself."

"When did you last see Sixto?"

"We was trimming some of those wild plum bushes in the front on Wednesday…we finished about 4:30 then I took off. Last time I seen Sixto he was heading back to the shed."

"The shed where he was found?"

"Yeah, that's the only shed we got. I got all my stuff in there: you know when I can go in? I gotta get my computer."

"What kind of computer do you have?"

"Macbook Pro. I store my scheduling stuff on it— when to trim the wild plum bushes, when to pinch the Bloodflowers, when to turn on the drip for the Painted Daisies—it's not easy to keep track of all that."

"So that's your computer they found in the shed?"

About ten, ah, maybe five years ago, I stopped hating every attractive woman younger than me. I regressed for Lowenthal's secretary. She was about thirty, tastefully bedecked in a dark blue Max Mara skirt suit with expensive blue Marni platform sandals: she wore it all all too well.

"Thank you for seeing me, Mr. Lowenthal. I know this has been a difficult time for you."

"Police cooperation is a vital element of a civilized society; provided, of course, that the police deserve such cooperation and such cooperation is not abused."

"Now sitting here in your lovely home, rather than coming downtown on a hot summer day, that can hardly be counted as abuse, now can it Mr. Lowenthal?" That was rude, and a mistake: the man had lost his wife less than four months ago.

His eyes narrowed and his lips pursed. "It's not a given that I would *come downtown* to answer any questions regarding a suicide."

"Mr. Lowenthal, I apologize for my discourtesy. Let's start again, shall we?"

"What is there to say? Sixto killed himself."

"You and I both know that's not true. How long did Sixto work here?"

"You are very presumptuous about many things. I should think such presumption might prevent you from reaching satisfying conclusions to your various inquiries. I don't know that Sixto didn't kill himself, and I don't know how long he worked here: you'll need obtain that information from Mr. Samuels or Ms. Zemlinsky."

"Yeah it's my computer, and they won't let me have it: can you see about that for me?"

"Why would Sixto write a suicide note on your computer?"

"Fuck I know, pardon my French. I didn't hang with the guy. Probably because it was there, to answer your question."

"Do you always keep it in the shed?"

"No, I usually carry it around with me in my backpack. But when I'm chopping or something, I put it in the shed to charge it."

"And you're not afraid something will happen to it?"

"The shed's got a lock, and there ain't too many people wandering around the grounds. The inside help stays inside, so it's usually just me and Sixto. The grounds and house all have cameras too. Besides," he smiled smugly, deluded into thinking he possessed something in this universe to be smug about, "I put one of those password protections on it: even if some lowlife did lift it, he couldn't use it."

"The grounds and house have surveillance cameras?"

"Mr. Lowenthal's big on security."

"Did Sixto have a key to the shed?"

"Yeah, he needed one."

"Sixto and me, we go way back. Cañon City, before, we both got kicked out of East, then the army. Sixto was good people."

"Sixto sold narcotics, Mr. Bratsche, and did hard time. Call me old-fashioned, but some do not consider a convicted felon dope peddler 'good people.'"

"You're smarter than that Ma'am, Detective. There's good folks in prison, and..." he looked around the urine-scented room, "bad folks in police stations."

"*Touché*, Mr. Bratsche. When did you last see Sixto?"

"Two, three weeks ago. He came to my place, we had a couple a beers, shot the shit. And that was it."

"What day and time exactly, Mr. Bratsche?"

"Must have been Tuesday, or Wednesday, no Tuesday, definitely Tuesday. It was eleven, eleven thirty. He left kind of abrupt, you know, said he had to be someplace at midnight."

"That's the way he said it, he had to be 'someplace at midnight'? He wasn't going home, in other words?"

"No, he wasn't going home."

"Did he smoke a lot of dope, Mrs. Gonsalvo? Was he selling drugs again?"

"*Estúpida gringa*," under her breath: "No, no Detective he liked his *grass,* his *lawn,* the flowers and shit, being outside. Sixto loved that job, he couldn't wait to get to work in the A.M."

"How long did he work there?"

"About a year. Right out of Cañon. Some cop set it up for him before he got out, I think."

"A police officer set it up for him?"

"Or maybe it was his parole officer, I don't know. You all the same to me."

"So Sixto was happy, you'd say, with his job, with you, with his life in general?"

"Yeah. No way he killed himself, no way."

"No money problems?"

"We was ok. He even got a big bonus last spring."

"How involved are you in hiring your help, Mr. Lowenthal?"

"I'm not at all involved. Ms. Zemlinsky takes care of all of that."

"So Ms. Zemlinsky oversees the hiring and firing of your domestic staff?"

"I have final approval, but that is one of her duties, yes."

"I find it odd, Mr. Lowenthal, that you'd approve the hiring of an ex-con, a convicted drug pusher, to a position where he'd have access to at least the grounds, and possibly more, of your estate."

"I trust Ms. Zemlinsky implicitly."

"But you were aware of Mr. Gonsalvo's criminal record?"

"Of course."

"When were you aware?"

"I don't understand."

"At what point in the hiring process were you made aware that Mr. Gonsalvo was a convicted drug felon?"

"Before he was hired. Ms. Zemlinsky informed us, while Sixto was still imprisoned, I believe, that he would be an excellent candidate for the recently vacated assistant gardener position. We looked at his application, had a very brief discussion, and agreed."

"You said 'we' and 'us': who else was involved?"

"Your questions are becoming tedious, Detective Fruscella."

"Working late tonight, Detective?"

"These fucking interviews, too much doesn't make sense. I haven't even started looking at your Dehmel stuff yet."

"So what doesn't fit?"

I looked up at him, "'Sixto killed himself,' that's what you told me. There's no murder, and so no murder investigation. How can we talk about what doesn't exist?"

He shrugged, "How can you be so sure someone killed him?"

"Like I said, too much doesn't make sense: like why someone would try to make it look like a suicide."

"You don't think it was a suicide because it looks like a suicide? That's all you got?"

"Don't you have your own case to solve? I seem to remember hearing something like 'I don't want or need your help.'"

"I'd like your files soon."

"I'll have someone send them over tomorrow."

"You say he received a bonus last spring: do you know how much he received?"

"Five thousand dollars."

"Mr. Lowenthal wrote Sixto a check for five thousand dollars?"

"I didn't see no check. Sixto gave me ten Ben Franklins, told me to buy something nice, not to use it on bills or nothing, cuz he got this big bonus at work for making the flowers grow and the grass green."

"Do you remember the date?"

"I sure do: April 21st."

"So Sixto was given a bonus *before* the real garden work began?"

"Garden work goes on all year round. I know what you thinking," she gave me a little nod with her chin. "You thinking that he got that money from some shady business, from selling dope or something, that's what you thinking."

"Did Sixto spend a lot of time at home after work?"

"What do you mean?"

"After he left work, did he come home to you, or did he

go out with friends, or did he come home to you and then go out with friends, or did you go out together?"

"Me and Sixto, we had something good together. He wasn't stepping out on me."

"I'm very glad to hear that, but if I'm going to find out who killed him, I'll need to know where and with whom he spent his time."

"You know, Mr. Lowenthal, when someone refuses to answer a question, it piques my curiosity and makes me suspect that that someone is trying to hide something important."

"Detective, I am attempting to remain patient in the face of your unfounded, insulting and quite frankly rather *outré* hallucinations. I cannot understand, however, the possible bearing the circumstances of Gonsalvo's hiring could have on his suicide, some months after the fact."

"The more you refuse to answer this question the more certain I am of its importance."

"'*Le doute n'est pas une condition agréable, mais la certitude est absurde,*' pardon my French."

I closed my notebook and shifted forward in my seat. "Mr. Lowenthal, I can be absurdly disagreeable, more than you can possibly imagine. Presently, I am trying to make this as easy as possible for you, but if you don't answer this question immediately, my tactics will change."

"But what are your tactics and threats to me, Detective? I should think neither your superiors nor the public would encourage the persecution of a man who has just suffered the brutal murder of his wife."

I stood, "Please be at Denver Police Headquarters at 1331 Cherokee street at 3 pm this afternoon."

"I could have you removed from this case with a single telephone call."

"That's terrible dialogue. Perhaps you should try it in French."

"I detest self-righteousness."

"And I detest hypocrisy. I can't understand how a man who built a public a career advocating maximum criminal sentencing and the deportation of immigrants..."

"*Illegal* immigrants, Detective Fruscella, *illegal* immigrants..."

"Did Sixto know the password to your computer?"

He shook his head, "No way."

"Do you usually leave your computer in the shed when you leave in the afternoon?"

"Depends on where I am. If I'm down near the pond or on the north side, I'll just get on my bike and scoot. If I'm near the shed, I'll stick it in my pack first."

"Did you lock your computer, with the password protections and all, before you left that day?"

"Probably. I think so."

"But you can't be certain?" He shrugged. "Leaving aside the computer for a moment, did Sixto seemed depressed or anything that Wednesday?"

"No clue. He had his Mexican radio, you know, and I got my earbuds. We didn't talk much."

"Did you ever see Sixto with anyone else? His wife perhaps, or a friend?"

"No, I never seen him with nobody."

"Did you ever see anyone drop him off or pick him up from work?"

"I never seen Sixto with nobody. We don't have too many Mexicans, Hispanics around here: most of the inside help is Oriental, and I'm the only other gardener, and the driver, the driver's another white guy with a funny accent."

"Do you remember who introduced you to Mr. Gonsalvo when he was hired?"

"Yeah, I was working on some rose trellises and him and Zemlinsky came out of the garage. She said 'Here's your new helper, Sixto' and we put up the trellises the rest of the day."

"Why didn't you tell me you were the arresting officer at one of Sixto's drug busts? The one that got him sent up?"

"It was Birk's collar. I was just along for the ride. We were actually after whatsisname, his boss, Hemple, and Sixto got in the way."

"You testified, right?"

"I think so...what's it say there?"

"Yeah, you both did. What's Birk doing now?"

"He retired to Montana or someplace, no, definitely Wyoming, Jackson Hole I think: some of the Narco guys still keep in touch, like DeRose and Miller."

"When did he retire?"

"Sometime after I left. Why?"

"Do you know Sixto's PO, Kelling?"

"Heard he's a hard-ass, but never met him personally. Why?"

"Sixto's wife told me some cop helped him get the job with Lowenthal. I'm just trying to figure out who that cop could be."

"A cop set it up for him?"

"That's what she said."

"She's probably lying."

"Do you know where he was going, Mr. Bratsche… girlfriend, dealer, bookie? I'm guessing he didn't have an appointment with his PO, and Lowenthal's flowers don't require midnight watering."

"I don't know where he was going, Detective. He never told me. He just said 'he had to be someplace at midnight,' and then split."

"How about an educated guess?"

"I picked up my diploma at Cañon City, Detective, and Cañon City taught me to keep my guesses to myself."

"C'mon, Mr. Bratsche, you must have some idea. There's nothing here to protect: my interest is focused exclusively on Sixto's nocturnal whereabouts, and any parole violations or other misdemeanor infringements are completely uninteresting to me and to this investigation."

"I got nothing to hide and I've no idea where he went."

"Do you know how Sixto got his job at Lowenthal's, Mr. Bratsche?" I mean it's not every day that a man walks straight out of a Cañon City Max cell into a Cherry Creek garden."

"You don't believe everything you hear."

"But you did hear something?"

"I heard he got some help."

"From whom? Kelling?"

"Kelling? That prick wouldn't piss on you if your head was on fire."

"...*illegal* immigrants, okay, would employ an ex-con Hispanic drug-dealer fresh out of the penitentiary. I can't wrap my head around the fact that, given who you are and everything you appear to represent, that you'd allow, let alone invite, such a character with a past like Sixto's within miles of your wife and hearth."

"Your hypocrisy astounds, Detective. Your *faux* concern for the ex-con Hispanic garden worker fools no one: you'd remain happily and forever oblivious to the poor man's death if he weren't somehow connected to me. Tell me, if his body were discovered in some Sun Valley third floor apartment bathtub or floating face down in the Platte near Valverde Park, would Denver's finest homicide detective be squaring her jaw, grim determination seeping from her furrowed brow, vowing at whatever cost to uncover the truth and see justice done? Would the physical evidence, the pistol in hand and suicide note, be so readily ignored? Would the all-too-obvious scenario, the venue of a self-inflicted death, be so quickly discarded in favor a hobby-horse ride to God knows where? So spare me your *teatro bufo* tears, Detective, your concern for Mr. Sixto is insincere and purely theoretical."

"Your command of rhetoric is impressive, Mr. Lowenthal, and I'm beginning to understand how comforting and persuasive your language might be to those who are, shall we say, less critically aware. The fact remains, however, that your beautiful and elegant language is primarily obfuscation. Your lengthy cadenzas signal to me that you're either stalling, or that you have no intention of answering these questions. Now some of this reluctance might be due to an inflated sense of self, a feeling of being above the law, and some of this might be traceable to a genuine desire to hide and deceive. So far, I've interpreted this performance as the manifestation of an egotistical and rather wordy asshole, pardon *my* French, and I've found the best way to deal with egos such as your own is to wait them out, give them enough rope, and they'll usually take it, and, if not hang themselves, then at least trip themselves up. But maybe there is a method to your madness; maybe you are genuinely trying to hide something. Maybe it's political, maybe you think that given your ideology, hiring a diverse staff, including an ex-con Hispanic, might appeal. Or maybe it's something else."

"Why would she lie?"

"Fuck I know, get back at the po-lease."

"I don't know, I don't think so. This whole hiring thing doesn't fit together. Right out of Cañon, he walks into Lowenthal's garden. There's something shady in this garden, Benderson, something shady. I need to talk to that secretary, Zemlinsky."

"Didn't you interview her already?"

"No, Ramirez did. I can't find the file. You talk to her last summer?"

"Yeah, file should be there. Why do you think there's something shady?"

"Don't be dense: how the fuck did Sixto get that job? Someone had to set it up for him: the question is who? Mrs. Sixto thinks some cop, and that makes sense. Zemlinsky didn't put a help-wanted ad in the *Cañon City Times*, so how'd she know to hire the guy?"

"Birk?"

"I don't know any Birk."

"Mr. Bratsche, I can think of only a few reasons that a police officer would help a convict obtain a job on the outside, and of those that don't include sexual favors, all involve some sort of snitching. Snitching might explain Sixto's mysterious nocturnal wanderings, as well as his premature and unnatural demise. I repeat that I'm not at all interested in passing judgment on Sixto's character or behavior, but the identity of Sixto's acquaintances, especially this helpful police officer, seems key. Imagine, just imagine, Mr. Bratsche, how the knowledge of the name of this officer could advance my case. And how the withholding of this name might make me impatient."

He looked around the room, then at the mirror behind me. "You already have the answer, Detective."

"I don't understand. What do you mean, I already have the answer?"

"I'm no rat, I keep my mouth shut."

"But Sixto *was* a rat: all I'm asking is for whom did he squeal?"

He shrugged.

"You said I already have the answer: it wasn't Birk, and it wasn't Kelling…" I froze. "Benderson?"

*　*　*

"He was with me most of the time. Like I said, we were getting along good."

"But he wasn't with you all of the time."

"No, he went to see his buddies, whatshisname, the guy he was in Cañon with, Brats."

"Mr. Cornelius Bratsche. Anybody else?"

"That's all I know."

"How often did he get together with Mr. Bratsche?"

"Two times a week, sometimes three. Tuesday, Friday, sometimes Sunday. Saturday night was my night."

"Where he'd take you?"

"To the 'Pec, the Chapultepec. He liked jazz."

"Going to a nightclub or bar is a parole violation. Wasn't he afraid of getting caught and sent back?"

"Said no worries, said he was cool, at least at the 'Pec."

"What did he man by that, that 'he was cool'?"

"I don't know. I ain't like you, I don't ask all these questions, I just try to enjoy life, know what I'm saying?"

"Did you ever talk to Sixto, get to know anything about him?"

"What do you mean?"

"I don't know, talk about sports, women, whatever two men talk about when they're trimming bushes or killing weeds together."

"No, like I said, I have my earbuds and he had his radio. It's about time for me to knock off, is this going to take longer?"

"I still have a few questions, yes. Did you recommend Sixto for his bonus in April?"

"Bonus, what bonus? We didn't get no bonus."

"Sixto's wife said he received a five thousand dollar bonus in April. This is news to you?"

"Lowenthal don't give bonuses."

"Maybe Zemlinsky gave it to him without Lowenthal knowing?"

"If money's going out, Lowenthal knows about it. We don't get nothing here, not even a bottle at Christmas or the Kippers or whatever. We got time cards too, and overtime don't exist."

"Why the fuck didn't you tell me Sixto was your grinder?"

"Oh Jesus Christ."

"This is bad, this is fucking bad. You are so screwed."

"I'll fix it, don't worry, I'll fix it."

"HOW? How are you going to fix it? You don't tell me that a murder victim whose case I'm investigating is your grinder? You think I wouldn't find out? What kind of detective do you think I am?"

"I was just trying to buy some time."

"I don't fucking care. I have nothing to say to you. I can't even stand to be in the same room. I want a statement detailing your relationship with Sixto, from the very beginning. I want *all* pertinent files and docs included. I want everything tomorrow morning."

"Can I predate my statement?"

"Let's go back to Sixto's hire. Mr. Gonsalvo was employed

as a replacement for your previous assistant, is that correct?"

"I didn't have no previous assistant. Sixto was the first."

"So there wasn't an advertised vacancy or anything like that?"

"Nope, not that I know of."

"Did you require assistance? Was it a two-person job?"

"No, I didn't need nobody. If there was some heavy lifting or something, which was rare, I'd go get Dmitri, that's the driver, and we'd handle it. I don't know why they needed the dude, Sixto, but I ain't the one making decisions." He looked behind me. "It's going to be kind of creepy, you know, that shed all shot up, and using that computer. I didn't know the dude or anything, but shit, that's a nasty way to buy it, spreading your fucking brains all over the wall of some shack full of manure and plant food. It makes you stop and think, you know?"

I refrained from comment and closed my notebook.

"I'm not going to have to clean that shed, am I? They got people who do that professionally, right?"

"I was with my wife, Detective, I was with my wife. We were discussing something in my office when Ms. Zemlinsky came in with two or three minor questions and tasks concerning this home. She was fortunate to catch us together, as my wife always made it a point to involve herself as much as possible in management of our household, and domestic decisions made in her absence sometimes had to be reconsidered. Ms. Zemlinsky suggested we needed a gardener's helper, my wife asked if she had anyone in mind, and Ms. Zemlinsky presented us with a folder and résumé of your Mr. Gonsalvo. I don't remember any discussion, my wife seemed satisfied, so we moved on to other issues."

"Did your wife look at the folder?"

"I assume so."

"Did you?"

"I honestly don't remember. It was not a momentous occasion, Detective."

"Did Ms. Zemlinsky's folder include any personal references, Mr. Lowenthal? Any note from Sixto's parole officer, or another member of the police force?"

"No, not that I remember."

"Where's the folder now?"

"I assume Ms. Zemlinsky has it."

"I understand you have surveillance cameras installed in the house and around the grounds: I'd like to look at some of those recent tapes."

"Of course Detective: I'll be happy to show the you the discs. When you show me a warrant."

He shrugged and looked at his hands on the table.

"Mr. Bratsche, was it Detective Benderson who helped Sixto get his job?"

He looked up at me, then back at his hands.

"It's extremely important to know how to read silences, Mr. Bratsche. I think that's probably one thing detectives and prisoners have in common, at least good detectives and good prisoners, the ability to understand quiet, stillness, rests." I paused, looked at the Sergeant, then at Bratsche.

"Did you hear any of this, of this arrangement, from Sixto, Mr. Brastche?"

"No Ma'am, he never talked about it, never said word one. For obvious reasons."

"For obvious reason indeed. For if word got around the yard that Sixto was a snitch, the general prison population wouldn't be too pleased, would they Mr. Bratsche? And if word got out on the street that Sixto was grinding, there would be those who would also wish Sixto harm, wouldn't there, Mr. Bratsche? Sixto's grinding might be, what we police detectives call, *a motive* for his murder. My question to you, Mr. Bratsche, is what was your role in all of this? You must have been torn, torn between your loyalty to your 'good people' friend from high school and the moral code of prisoners and criminals when it comes to informants and rats. Were you complicit in this arrangement, maybe included by either Sixto or Benderson, to share the bounty? Or were you biding your time, perhaps waiting for an opportune moment to confront Sixto and perhaps extract some sort of payment or revenge for his dime dropping and grinding? Are you a suspect in this murder, Mr. Bratsche?"

"No, perhaps we are not alike, Ms. Gonsalvo, perhaps we are not all alike. I am curious about why you were not: why you never thought to question how Sixto got a such a plum job directly out of prison; why you never wondered how he earned a five grand cash bonus after eight months; and why you never asked how he could go to bars and nightclubs, in direct violation of his parole, without worry or concern. And you tell me you thought a police or parole officer helped him with all this. What does this all add up to for you?"

"I don't know what you're saying."

"I'm saying that Sixto was a snitch, Ms. Gonsalvo: that's why he was paroled early; that's why he was given a job at Lowenthal's; that's likely the origin of his bonus and that's how he was allowed to party at the 'Pec. And that's probably why he was killed."

"The fuck you talking, Sixto being a snitch? You just guessing now, lady."

"In the absence of other explanations, this at least seems possible. Can you think of another reason he'd be killed?"

"You need to ask that cop. Ask that cop who helped him!"

"When I discover who it was, I will. Did Sixto have other enemies, enemies from before he was sent up? He kept his mouth shut then, during the trial, didn't he? I don't remember any deal with the DA, in fact, he got the max because he wouldn't cooperate. Do you know of anything that may have changed his mind?"

They all were lying, they all were hiding something. Like bad transcriptions, the facts were there, but nothing sounded right. Lowenthal was probably the worst: he hit the right notes but it was obvious he was straining, like a contralto trying to keep above the staff, or a coloratura doing contemporary, Callas singing Berg. And what was Benderson thinking? This was bad, this was fucking bad. Why did he need a grinder for Crimes Against Persons? Was he still working Narc? If he failed to disclose any contact with Lowenthal before his wife's murder he'd be done as a cop. Probably do time too. And why lie so stupidly to me? He had to know I'd find out; did he want me to find out? I'd read his statement, but I'd still need to go to Schlaf to cover my ass. I needed to talk to that secretary, Zemlinsky, and maybe look at some of those surveillance tapes. This was bad, this was so fucking bad.

CHAPTER 5

Fünf Klavierstücke
op. 23

III. langsam

The dumpster was polished, spotless. Although aged, its sides and floor sparkled. Purity spoiled by Benderson's corpse. Almost amused, his eyes and mouth smiled. The wounds were large, brutal. Body surrounded by 1000-Peso notes. His clothes folded, immaculate, unscathed. Upon recycling bin, suit and underwear arranged. Shoes shined beneath shirt, tie. The site felt staged, theatrical. Completely wrong, Benderson's body and background mocked.

The sun rose over suburban strip mall, police and investigators gathered, outraged, vengeful. Not popular, the victim was nevertheless police, his murder and sepulture rankled. The coroner examined, hands probing with tenderness, care, expert, painstaking. I walked back to the dumpster, saw final broken body, face.

"Wasn't killed here, obviously. Got a time of death for me?"

"I don't know: six hours ago? Give or take fifteen." He pointed to one of the wounds on his chest, "Four entry wounds from Black Talon cop-killers, from a .40 Smith and Wesson fired at relatively close range, say less than three feet. He was dead before he hit the ground, Detective."

"The body looks awfully clean."

"They scrubbed around all wounds. The killers washed with full-spectrum medical rub, and they were extremely thorough."

"Extremely strange: this is like opera, *Magic Flute, La Bohème*, because it exaggerates. Everything points to a meat eater executed; nude sanitized body, pesos." I walked around the dumpster, thinking: excessive, stylized, Benderson, Lowenthal. This was all histrionic: not revenge or warning—silencing was the point here. Like this, no dealer murders, careful, meticulous, all details and props measured. This scene was like Sixto's, where surfaces and appearances were melodramatic, mendacious. The cases were analogous, connected. With possible Dehmel murder and Benderson link. I walked to alley's edge. Above crowded inviting Starbucks, the sun rose.

The day would be bright, hot.

CHAPTER 6

Erwartung
Monodram op. 17

To want to forget. To walk down the stairs quietly a bottle of Johnnie Black and a glass full of ice in hand. To be numb to not think yet to not think ever to be able to not think to forget. With music. To hear music and to try to be able to forget. To see the moon to shine in from the window and to be able to see the door and lock and easily to insert the key and to open the door and to step through. To have no thoughts no thoughts yet no thoughts of lifeless eyes or cold limbs or dumpsters and bloodless wounds. To have no thoughts of the past no memories not yet.

The back room to be dark and to feel the way carefully to pass the work stool and the corner of the bench to pass the front counter and to stand on the thick carpet of the foyer. The moon to disappear. To do not turn the lights on to do not to want any light other than the moon. To walk through the door of the first and nearest studio and to silently close the door behind. There to be no window no moon no light. To blink. To move cautiously by feel to the far wall not to count steps but to walk slowly so as to be able to stop immediately. To feel and then to kneel down to place the glass down on the floor and to reach out to touch to touch. To feel the cool metal and then to find the switches and to push or to flip. Fingertips to move up and down the smooth metal and glass to turn on switch by switch to see the soft glimmer of the red and green and below the orange glow of the tubes. To hear the faintest hum. To move slightly right and to repeat the process a little easier because of the faint glow recently illumed. To see just enough the second rack of darkened boxes and to bring these to light a soft warm luster and a slight smell the smell of new clean metal and glass.

To bend down to see. To press buttons methodically one two three four and to hope. To listen and to hear nothing still. To press other buttons more combinations without haste until to hear a soft piano the melancholy trills of the *Sarabande* of Bach's *French Suite #6 in E major* Angela Hewitt. To turn knobs press buttons to get more volume greater more. To find glass with ice to shuffle on knees back to the listening chair to sit and to pour. To not yet think to not yet remember to not yet acknowledge.

To enjoy the luxury of discontinuity disintegration randomness. To refuse narrative to take every event as a discrete entity an unconnected fragment a simple phenomenon without origin or legacy temporarily. To allow only *that* quarter note C♯ minor chord *that* taste of smoky whisky *that* blurred glimmer of red and green diodes with the orange smear beneath. With effort. To forget. With effort. To maintain absolute now. For now. For how long? When?

To listen. To listen to hear and to hear to invite time into the room. To hear the perfect authentic cadence and the A to resolve inevitably inexorably inescapably to the E. To remember. Not to remember necessarily but to have memory time to intrude. To have time to interrupt. To remove the pedal to allow the chord to die. A meaningful death. A meaningful stillness a quiet a rest *fortissimo*. To hear unavoidably meaning within the stillness. And the light staccato of the *Gavotte* to begin to dance and to mock.

To kiss those lips not cold. To feel those arms not stiff. To run tongue over that chest not wounded. To not be sure if to love but to be certain of what? To be certain to remember that memory and certainty can never to coexist. But to laugh and to live together some twenty five years before out of the Academy. Before husband before child before homicide before detective before Crimes Against Persons before Dehmel before Sixto before dumpster. Before another drink and to hear the ice to clink over French trills.

On blistery summer days to mix sweat spit and other juices in shared small one bedroom Cap Hill apartment when crack was just to start to hit and Colfax to be truly nasty from Broadway all the way to Aurora and beyond. To walk out never alone in the finally cool three am air to the bodega for popsicles or orange juice or Marlboros and to step over the almost insentient bodies to sprawl against the bricks hand on weapon head on swivel no laughing no talking no drill the shadows alive. To fall back in bed after to laugh and to kiss and to smoke in the dark to feel important and invulnerable and possible. To nearly remember the taste of mouth the smell of armpits the upward curve of dick the blondish hair on chest the small sigh always to hear when to come and to have memories all now to change to corrupt to ruin by the clean dumpster the peso bills the scrubbed body and open eyes. More more twenty five years of blood of shit of skin to puncture by bullet blade stick and bottle of throat to throttle by hands rope wire and cloth of bones to crush by metal wood stone and brick of to force outside inside and inside outside all all to come between bedroom and alley clothes thrown and clothes folded Marlboros and Black Talons rumpled bed and immaculate dumpster. Sadly. Another drink the glass now to be mostly ice.

The *Gavotte* to end abruptly clinically and the *Polonaise* to begin alike. Bach's precision pleasing comforting to resist the chaos of the world.

No big argument no falling apart just a not gradual drifting a separating to begin twenty five years ago and to continue until this morning. A very long time and a very long way. The final recent encounters fraught tense impolite stupid but atypical. Obviously mistrust and something to hide. Nothing as dramatic or as anomalous before. No definite scene to mark the end at least none to remember. Transfers conflicting shifts an expiring lease no recollected affairs but unsure and ultimately not to matter. To discuss once or twice with calm and sweetness *tranquilo dolce* and to finally live alone and to meet and to go with and to fuck others and to meet and to go with and to fuck and to marry husband Roberto. And to give birth to Nicholas. And to forget Benderson at first gradually but then swiftly with greater and greater momentum until quickly and finally almost completely. But not completely. Obviously.

Roberto dead to die in a car accident. Some of Roberto to be forgotten as well.

But Nicholas around to grow and to remind. To not to be able to think about Roberto without to think about Nicholas. Sadly. But Roberto's body not to be seen *in situ* to mangle in steel and glass but to be viewed only in funeral home already to clean and to rearrange to reconstruct. Not to forget Benderson's body also not to find on site also to clean and to rearrange. Significant. Still infinitely different.

To think to remember to recall to recapture what? The self before? Before all the blood and shit and tears and now age? Before the stiffening joints the wrinkling skin the sagging breasts and the drying cunt? Not completely not to finish not yet. But still. On the way. To remember to be to slow to delay to postpone? To deny? To ignore? To recapture the before to be to forget the now. No. Not to be able to ignore to forget. Impossible. To remember the before to be not to be able to forget the now. Obviously.

To remember then to be to desire what? To hope to gain what? To remember to be to what advantage? If to recapture the before to remember to be not to be able to forget the now then to what point to be to remember? To reconstruct? To reconstruct a before self but a before self always to taint by the memory of the now self. This pure before self never to be always to be a false self untrue impossible. To remember then to be to recreate? Or to create more precisely. To remember then to be to create a self never to be. To what point? To feel better. Obviously. But how?

Memories of Benderson to dissolve in memories of others. And perhaps dreams or snatches of images or information of others. The after hours FoxHole dancing back when LoDo to be sketchy warehouses and the sun to always surprise. To be really Benderson? Dinner at Patsy's low candlelight and cheap wine to be really Benderson? To ski at Eldora and a long snowball fight with friends in Nederland. With Benderson? Possibly. Likely. But not certainly.

The *Polonaise* to end and the *Bourrée* to begin. Relentless eighth notes. The *French Suites* to be too quick even with Hewitt to take the repeats. To want something slower longer something to be able to concentrate upon. Maybe a *Toccata* although the harpsichord and organ to be to avoid. Or a fugue for a fugue state. *Italian Concerto*? *French Overture*? To mean to rise to search to maybe turn on lights and to forage but what chances of a Gould's *Toccata and Inventions* or a Rangell or another Hewitt to be found? Not to mention Tureck although not quite in the mood for all that expression. The Richter *Toccata and Fugue* to be obvious certainly a common piece to show off the bass capabilities. To remain to sit and to listen to the *Bourrée* and to try to not feel. Sick.

To remember a new small lamp above a rack to the right and to decide quickly to rise and to seek. To replace cap on bottle and to set down on the carpet and then to get up and to walk slowly to the right left hand to extend forward to search. A couple of steps slightly to illuminate by the equipment. To stop and to wave hand to the left towards the vague dark shapes and to find the lamp and to switch on. To see the top of the glass rack and four of five neatly stacked CDs with Ellington and Brown's *This One's for*

Blanton! on top as well as three or four fanned LPs in their covers Miles Davis *Kind of Blue* Wynton Marsalis *Standard Time Volume I* The Allman Brothers *Eat a Peach* and *The Three Tenors in Concert*. No thanks to be not in the mood for jazz or bombast and to be not sure of how to work the turntables anyway. To set the glass down. Maybe something underneath the Ellington Gotan Project *La Revancha del Tango* Dave Matthews *Crash* Alicia Keys *As I Am* Alfred Brendel *The Art of Alfred Brendel I* and Shania Twain *Come On Over*. To take the Brendel and to replace the stack to take the glass now mostly water and to switch the lamp off and to move slowly effortlessly to the left. To hear the *Bourrée* and its maddening eighth notes end the *Meneut* to begin quickly mercifully. To kneel down in front of the rack and to press buttons to stop the Bach in mid trill to eject and to remove and to insert and to play and to hear Haydn's *Andante con Variazioni* to remember an early recital middle school maybe Young Musicians Competition Pueblo Central High School Auditorium to dress up to wear Lia's good blouse mama's pearl earrings to play poorly to misfinger most of the arpeggios in the trio and to totally fuck the triplets near the final repeat. To turn and to move back to the chair. To sit and to lean and to feel around for the bottle to find quickly to take and to pour and to drink as Brendel to trill the Gb major chord and then to lightly touch the descending dotted thirty second sixty fourth notes before the beginning of the *Trio*.

The afternoon dark living room on Thatcher where to sit up straight and not to wince and to listen to Mrs. Domica to count one two three four and to sometimes nod with closed eyes a facial expression of aesthetic joy too weird and gross to favorably impress a young Pueblo girl of twelve. To accidently break a teacup one day to knock it off with books in arm and to cry and to shake until the lesson to abandon and to be necessary to call mother. To hear the bark of softer softer echo through the close room and to startle to break concentration and to be to force to begin again from the repeat. Always from the repeat. To be able to get away with some sloppiness with Mrs. Domica to use heavy pedal with Chopin and to rubato Mozart unmercifully. To wonder if Mrs. Domica's lack of teaching talent to cause own lack of performance talent or reverse. To covet Mrs. Domica's Bechstein upright and to wonder where it to be now.

To realize the need to stop to think about the past and to focus on the present and future. Or to be more precise to think about the past only in relation to the present and future. Or to be more precise to think abut Benderson and Benderson's death instead of to focus on how Benderson and Benderson's death to affect the self. Or to be more precise to think about Benderson and Benderson's death only in order to solve Benderson's death irrespective of self. Or to be more precise to think about Benderson and Benderson's death in relation to self only when this relation would help to answer the questions of Benderson's death and to not think about the relation when no help to be to find. To reimagine the white board at the office with a photograph of Benderson to stick on top above a photo of Sixto above a photo of Dehmel. To draw three black whiteboard marker lines to connect the three photographs to a photograph of Lowenthal although the line to connect the Lowenthal photo to the Benderson photograph to be dotted to signify the connection between Lowenthal and Benderson to be uncertain unproven. To be key. Obviously.

Benderson Sixto and Dehmel on the whiteboard like a triad a chord. A major or minor? Inverted? Benderson or Dehmel the root? Sixto important? Flatted or augmented? Sixto likely secondary not to be the main target minor flatted. Dehmel or Benderson Benderson or Dehmel? Inversion or root? Related but how? Lowenthal.

Brendel to go into the F major section of the first variation and to hear the thirty second note triplets and the sixty fourth note runs slightly more directed than trills to remember approximately obviously how they to appear on the page rests in the bass staff with thick triplets and then frantic sixty fourths to descend in the treble overhead. Then a repeat then a thirty second note run that to start in the left hand to continue in the right then to alternate until the minor finale. The pages thick with notes fingerings and slurs although the tempo fairly steady and minimal *crescendos* and *decrescendos* to be to remember. To be some time since to hear the *Andante* at one time to be a favorite. Perhaps to suggest to Nicholas who to like often the sad pieces.

To see or to think the notation on the page to be extremely different than to hear the music in the air just as to see the photographs on the board to be very different than to see the bodies to be now dead. To have the music in front in sight while to play seriously to be nearly impossible. To memorize to be necessary. To anticipate. Always. To see and to play what to be seen to be impossible. To see to mean not to hear and not to hear to make to play impossible. To see to be fine to rehearse but to see and to play seriously to be impossible. Gould to sing and to hear and to play. Or to hum at least. To play seriously to close one's eyes and to not see. Obviously. To not see the musical notation. But to not see the musical notation to be not to be the same as to not see the music as such. To see the music as such?

To shake the head and to take a small sip of whiskey. To remember to be able practice on a Bösendorfer in college to sneak into the auditorium courtesy of a potential boyfriend's key to practice the Brahms *Paganini* with nothing but a small music lamp in the piano black hall. To eventually switch the lamp off and to play with joy the notes to come from fingers hands and wrists mind to anticipate bars sometimes pages ahead. But to anticipate not to see the notes on the page not to see the fingers on keys but to hear what would to be to come. To anticipate. To expect. The future to be there. The past to be there. The present to be there. To see the notes not as notation but as sound as pieces of a pattern luminous to rise up from soundboard and to drift into the blackness. To see patterns lines actual shapes meaningful and ordered free and expressive. Finally not to see. To not see to hear and to know to be. Somehow. To see shapes and colors rare but to see nothing never again. Only that once.

To return to the matter at hand. To find a connection between Lowenthal and Benderson. To blacken the dotted line. Lowenthal the likely killer if the same for Benderson Sixto and Dehmel. But what if not the same what if some sort of upper class gang war then Lowenthal to become the possible victim? The next possible victim? Suspect or victim? Both? Wife then assistant gardener then what?

Benderson yes but Benderson to be what to Lowenthal? Wife killing not uncommon police killing rather uncommon but assistant gardener killing? Ex-con drug pusher informant killing? But not ex-con drug pusher informant to Lowenthal. Unless.

Sixto to sell drugs to Lowenthal? Not easy to believe. To be way too risky way too stupid. Maybe Sixto to sell something else to Lowenthal? Information for instance. What information could Sixto possibly to have or to gather to interest Lowenthal? Maybe Sixto to do other chores for Lowenthal.? To kill his wife for instance? Not an easy step from drug selling to hire killing marijuana to murder. Maybe everything to be possible now but to not think so. And Benderson? To fit in where? To kill a police officer to be a big deal not to be done lightly to bring police out of the woodwork. Inevitably. Did Sixto to know something? To pay off Sixto with bogus bonus? Then to kill him? Sixto to blackmail Lowenthal? But why to be to hire in the first place? Benderson. And the secretary Zemlinksy. To interview her personally as soon as possible tomorrow. At the police station. To take off gloves.

Already to listen as Brendel to proceed through the *Finale* the dotted thirty second sixty fourth figures repeating somberly mournfully majestically with slurred eighth notes in the left hand. To taste the now watery scotch still slightly smoky and to wish for more ice. Now the *accelerando* with a seeming echo in the bass but call and response both to play with the right hand and now to hear the sixty fourth note arpeggios harp like and magnificent and to think despite desire of Roberto to ride Lakeside roller coaster with an obviously distraught Nicholas age eight no idea as to why to think this now as the arpeggios *diminuendo et ritardando* the dotted thirty second sixty fourth note figure to return. To see Roberto and Nicholas to stand in line to wait and not to speak the son to not want to show fear the father to not want to demonstrate impatience or concern the mother to watch to only observe to be able to understand but not to share the line to move slowly the sun to be hot Nicholas to stare straight ahead at the back of some teenager and Roberto to look anywhere and everywhere except at Nicholas both to proceed slowly silently somberly among the sounds of fun machinery and the nauseous screams and raucous laughter of pre and post pubescent thrill seekers. The Haydn to attach itself to this remembered scene to conjure up and to become the soundtrack. Heads to bow Roberto and Nicholas both to shuffle through the shadowy gates to dutifully hand ticket to attendant and still to not look around to climb clumsily into car first Roberto then Nicholas as Brendel to reach the fermata just before the end the seat bar to push down to buckle both to stare again straight ahead like soldiers during drills or fresh prisoners. To shade eyes to feel sun to watch the car to rise into the sky up up until to reach the apex and to slow Brendel to descend now the left hand from F to FF and the cars to swiftly fall and the sun and the structure to make to see impossible to lower eyes to look around for shade to wait hear joyful screams to desire a bottle of water to end softly with four octave F's. Why Haydn?

Music to be like that whorish to be able to attach to everything anything to be able to attach and to fade to be able to attach and therefore to become unheard or if not completely unheard then nearly unheard background soundtrack accompaniment. To listen to music truly to mean to unattach disentangle forget at least on some level. To listen to hear music as such to mean to forget often at least on some level. The whimsical sixteenth notes of the *Allegro* of the *Piano Sonata in E flat* #49 to begin and to desire to recall the end of the scene to find shade and to wait and to look until to see first Roberto to walk loosely happily and to smile then to wave and to see Nicholas to giggle and to look at Roberto with an expression of appreciation not exactly of hopeful anticipation more precisely to not be an epiphany or in the big picture very significant at all but to be certainly or at least likely not to misremember. Roberto to die within the year and the look of hopeful anticipation to not be seen in Nicholas' eyes again. But why Haydn?

And why Benderson? And why Sixto? And why Dehmel? To take over the Dehmel case to insist. To be allowed to take over certainly. And the Benderson case obviously. To talk to Sergeant Owen to read the case files from the beginning to try to understand the relationship between Benderson and Lowenthal and Dehmel and the secretary Zemlinsky. And Sixto. To take another drink of whiskey and to wish for more ice and to worry about how to feel tomorrow morning.

To feel old at present. And alone. To not feel alone often to be too busy with work usually and to feel too grateful for son usually but now to feel alone and sorry. Unfair to lose a husband certainly obviously. To remember marriage to be not perfect to be able to recall real problems but real

problems not to be comparable to the sadness of to feel
alone. In the least. To ache in middle of chest and stomach.
To feel some slight trouble to breathe. Another drink of
watery whiskey to be no help. The syncopated eighth notes
of the Haydn to be no help. To stand suddenly likely no
help. Perhaps a walk. Where?

The murder to hit home. To not be an abstract prob-
lem of patterns but to hurt truly and personally. Tragically.
At least somewhat. To be now on both ends of the clichés
to both say and hear. To be to involve with a victim yes
a long time ago more but still. To argue face to face two
days ago. And to bury two days from now. To remember
recent exchanges tense and fraught. Leave now leave now
relentlessly insistently defensively unusually. To lie about involvement with the first murder Dehmel. And more. To lie
about involvement with Lowenthal and to lie about involvement with Sixto. To lie consistently unfailingly constantly.
Some lies stupid obvious to be to discover easily. Like the
lies about Sixto. Some lies less stupid less obvious less easy
to discover. Like the lies about Lowenthal and Dehmel.
Benderson not to be innocent to get in over head and to be
killed. Not to be killed by drug lord or some other bullshit
misdirection. To be killed in relation to murders of Dehmel
and Sixto. To be killed by Lowenthal?

Lowenthal likely not to be the type to be capable of
personally to put three cop killer bullets into Benderson.
Nor to be the type to be capable to cut Dehmel's throat to
shoot Sixto's brains out either. But to focus on the murder
of Benderson for now. Not to be able to assume certainly
that killer of Benderson to be the same as killer of Sixto to

be the same as killer of Dehmel. Lowenthal to have to hire another to murder face to face like that. Who? The other to murder face to face like that to have to be cold blooded and to be known by Benderson. Apparently close range no struggle. Probably but not certainly. To kill a cop to cost big bucks. Unless not to tell killer Benderson a cop. Unlikely that. To kill a cop and to undress and wash the body and to arrange the dumpster scene like that to require strange mind. Strange and expensive mind.

To not to be able to think too clearly. To sit to drink to listen to Haydn drunkenly tiredly miserably lonely. In the dark. To not be able to see the music as such. To be unable to see anything as such.

The *Allegro* abruptly to end. A motorcycle engine to race past outside loudly to startle. The *Adagio e cantabile* to begin sadly and slowly. The killing to end? To not know enough of the past and present to be able to anticipate. Not enough information to establish a pattern. Now cacophony an unknown and unknowable cadence. To return to what? Repeats possible. Certainly. Key signature as yet illegible form as yet unclear.

To set glass carefully on arm of chair and to unscrew cap of bottle and to pour attentively into glass hopefully not too much. To replace cap on bottle bottle on floor. To take another drink of scotch. To desire vaguely a cigarette although to quit ten or so years ago. To think about to walk upstairs to bed and to sleep. To be exhausted but to believe sleep impossible. To wish to have someone to talk to to feel that need. Not Nicholas obviously. Not Hector obviously. To feel that need for conversation for physical contact too.

Comfort. To be to comfort. Too much to ask? Evidently. To be too or not enough. To be old almost fifty. To be perhaps out of the game. To make decisions and to have those decisions to return to haunt. To bite in falling ass.

No decision to have husband to kill in car crash. No decision to have one time lover to kill in dumpster. To remember first days in Academy police instructor to say sometimes nothing to do sometimes life to be just a real motherfucker. Some lives to be more of a real motherfucker than others. To be drunk and self pitying to be no help. Still. To be alone in the dark to be no help. Alone? With Brendel and Haydn. To make what difference?

Haydn to keep Roberto alive? Bach to stop Benderson bullets? Brahms to prevent Dehmel throat cut? Beethoven to jam Sixto pistol? No. A tired monologue. A monodrama everpresent since college to reappear at moments of weakness or discouragement. Like now. To be ignored. If possible.

To tire of the Haydn honestly. To recognize the beauty and accomplishment of Haydn but to tire nonetheless. To prefer the *Andante con Variazioni* certainly to this Haydn sonata. To prefer the lucidity of Bach certainly even the *French Suites* even the *Italian Concerto* even with Alexandre Tharoud the Chopinista to Haydn except for the *Andante*. To love Haydn's String Quartets however especially the *Sunrise* and *Emperor*. To wish to hear the Emperor quartet the second movement especially instead of to listen to Brendel to play this Haydn sonata. Haydn as a rule too monophonic in the piano sonatas all the action to occur in the right hand while the left to simply chord or to simply keep rhythm. Except for the *Andante*. Not so the string quartets. This *adagio e can-tabile* winding down. Thankfully. To anticipate the final cadence. Yes. The *pianissimo* eighth note B♭ D one two three.

After a brief silence the faster *Menuet* to begin. To call for another drink of whisky. To now need to hear something else. To yawn. To be able to hear something else to require to rise from chair and to find something else to hear. Too much. To remember last lover to always hate that word lover to avoid it whenever possible and usually possible last what friend boyfriend fuck? To remember last boyfriend Lou same age about forty five twice divorced PD's office. Lou nice enough but to desire younger partner younger body younger mind to sometimes make too obvious. To initially find Lou's insistence on pre-sex showers and complete darkness if not charming then harmlessly quirky but soon to become annoying and finally insulting. To feel as if affair to be Lou's experiment to be nice guy. Lou to try to not pity but to not try hard enough. As much as possible. Lou easy to leave both to be relieved. And nothing since. And nothing to anticipate. Nothing to return to.

Brendel to take every fucking repeat repeats inside of repeats. Benderson's murder a threat to self how? To think about Benderson's and not own hole in chest. Benderson's holes physical own metaphoric. To think about physical rather than metaphoric actual rather than imagined objective rather than personal factual rather than emotional. To remember white board and to think Dehmel Sixto Benderson and to remember lines to connect with Lowenthal Benderson to be dotted. To remember Benderson's washed body. To suddenly need to stand and to leave. To stand quickly without bottle or glass and to turn from chair and to walk back back toward door and to walk out door. And to leave door open and to stand briefly before counter and to see moonlight. And to walk into workspace past workbench and to open door and to walk upstairs and to hear Brendel still to take repeats. Into the night. Infinitely.

CHAPTER 7

Fünf Klavierstücke
op. 23

IV. *schwungvoll*

The gardener's SUV was found, engine running. This annoying, blocking completely drop-off drive-though. Samuels' calloused hands handcuffed to wheel before dying. The thickish wrists cut deeply, splatters on leather seats, ruining and flamboyant. Tied tightly, feet constrained. The easy hypothesis: poisoning, asphyxiation.

Engine running, exhaust hose now removed, except for wrist and ankles, epidermis intact and unmarked. Killed ostentatiously. Warning. Threat. A graphic gesturing obviously. Perpetrator? Motive?

To whom was this addressed?

From whom did this originate?

The setting obviously important.

"You think this is weird?"

"Yeah: TOD?"

"I'd say five, five-thirty."

The immediate suspect Lowenthal. Killings connected. A relentless ostinato, inescapably. Germont guilty. Although hands unbloodied, guilty just the same. A panicked killing, obviously Lowenthal worried. And worried killers make mistakes without fail.

And overconfident detectives misidentify, fuck-ups beyond redeeming. It vital, to allow rigorously anomaly, discord into flexible hypothesis. I, distracted, met the CS officer abruptly. Face expressive.

"The victim's car arrived when?"

"Clerk from opposite 7-11 guesses about 5:00. She smokes always outside at 5:00. She saw the victim's vehicle."

"Accompaniment?"

"What?"

"Any other person? Passenger? Someone running away?" Exhausted, spent already. Brutality, theatrics, the goddam arrogance, cleverness: Lowenthal was no closer to stumbling perceptibly. Patterns present, but unheard. Noise, blood. I am no closer to proving, definitively, anything. Present, but unheard. Listen better, detective. Yes. Listen.

CHAPTER 8

Begleitmusik zu einer Lichtspielszene
(Drohende Gefahr, Angst, Katastrophe)
op. 34

I.

A Fed-Ex package sat ostentatiously on my cluttered desk, opened already. As the obvious question echoed loudly in my weary head: to understand causally concerning this Fed-exed arrival coinciding definitely with the homicidal warning, ignored evidently. In addition to the other possibility mistimed unfortunately between the received package mailed ignorantly toward the Samuel's murder. Relying obviously on the package's relevance. Talking loudly outside.

The sender's identity was obviously of a critical importance, promising—regardless of the dispatched contents—to indicate quickly, with some real doubt existing always beneath, the intended recipient, unwarned apparently, of the post-office killing. Peered hopefully at the sender's address inked carefully over and two disks shining comfortably inside. The black printing stipulating cleanly across an OFFICE-ENTRANCE CAMERA capitalized boldly above a spelled-out date. Wondered why, if these Lowenthal's discs, were separated seemingly by three months. Wondered why, apropos, the first date occurring just before the wife's murder. Wondered why, subsequent to, the second date occurring just before the Sixto "suicide." Noticed finally on the white envelope stuck firmly outside a blue form denoting publically that the affixed package had been received, officially, by one Sergeant Perez, dusted unsuccessfully for any latent prints, carried personally to the detective's office, delivered precisely at the nine o'clock hour.

Inserted curiously into the DVD player, leaned forward on the comfortable chair, watched tiredly as the various figures moved back and forth from the camera's left (date-stamped helpfully) to the camera's right returning sporadically to the camera's right (time-stamped as well beneath). Many unpopulated minutes followed inevitably until another unrecognized figure entered abruptly from the frame's edges moved obliviously to the other edge. Repeated indefinitely. Until?

II.

During nearly sleeping, eyes closed. A few in addition to desperately needed reinforcements sharp-eyed, all within quickly assembled team homicide, the near appropriately to be used room multi-media enough. Out of quickly extracted disc surveillance, these into carefully replaced envelope Fed-Ex, all out of—decisively moving—office dark, most.

Throughout, "Quickly gather team homicide, six, above to carefully watch discs Lowenthal, these from likely taken camera surveillance. Each above now hurry room media."

"What?"

"Into swiftly move room media, all."

"To carefully watch discs?"

"Correct."

"What?"

"By means of painstaking viewing, evidence detectable, that underneath possibly surfacing, suspect identified." The prior to desperately need coffee strong. Much.

"Before dutifully returning, we thorough most, outside, meticulously interviewed witnesses possible all to earlier asphyxiating killing, futilely. All concerning reportedly saw nothing. Dishonest? No."

"Despite completely handcuffed, Samuel's driver? No. Beside somehow driving, another necessary, yes. Alongside then vamoosed. Killer invisible?"

"No."

"From how flee site murder, then? To later return to interrogation neighborhood all."

"To likely related homicides previous, this?"

"Beyond even guessing."

"Coffee?"

"Sugared. A lot." Inside finally stepped room media, a few around variously scattered chairs plastic, three across horizontally arranged flat-screens huge the beneath patiently waiting equipment electronic. "Any about somewhat know equipment fucking all amidst here to work?" I impatient much.

Nearby enthusiastically raised hands several sufficient. Among tiredly was I imprecise most. "Into now insert DVD surveillance this in order to painstakingly watch monitors here all."

"For painstakingly look what?"

"Complete every of absolutely paying attention utter, the excluding consciously discounting nothing, rigorous. All regarding always speak, everything articulated, whatever in front of possibly see: we liberal, yes? For perfectly belonging—stranger, peculiar both. For conceivably can be anything useful, none concerning feasibly left out. Anyone perplexed? Yes?"

"For regardlessly articulate *everything* trivial, all?"

"Before recklessly ignore notions preconceived any. Besides, accurately determining unimportant knowable the from presently is impossibility." Quiet my for now would remain suspicions Lowenthal all among. "Now watch. We talkative a great deal of."

Opposite resolutely focusing door wooden, the beneath sometimes skipped digits time. "This below, why skipping time real?"

"These above possibly edited?"

"Camera motion-sensitive, a by likely triggered movement minute enough in front of."

"Possibly to miss something important?"

"Some. But when set detector smartly, these from continuously remain minutes thirty some by initially activated whatever."

"Sensitive?"

"Most from reliably activated insect large a. On obviously depends use desired the."

"In front of brusquely walking secretary Lowenthal, her across nicely moving, eyes pleasing the to."

"Stupidly talking."

"We loquacious. Your regarding sometime died sense humor."

"Your regarding never born intelligence baseline." Hers before initially interviewing? Benderson? Forgotten: a next quickly conduct follow-up secretarial. My against hopefully remain antipathy irrelevant all.

"Across slowly moving Conrad, senator, the alongside hotly strutting Zemlinsky."

"Ignored. The alongside obviously prefers buffets extensive, any, to lubriciously wiggling secretary."

"Lubricious no. Away naturally walks she exactly that."

"With lately party women willing any? Excluding habitually incarcerate? Download?"

"Jealous much?"

"Of?"

"Seriously, eating Conrad obsessed. One thousand above once spent Frasca Boulder. All without completely drinking. Wife skinny his with."

"How to spend wad large that on only eating?"

"Frasca pricey."

"Yes, but grossly to raven large boozeless a beyond impossibly to imagine. Frasca expensive, yes, but disgracefully."

"Connecting victims murder his concerning possibly know anyone?"

"Nonexistent."

An across suddenly strode man dark-suited, his over back-slicked hair gleaming, his towards purposefully gait aggressive. "A regarding possibly to identify?" Numbers visible, a before initially killing days seven. No followed significantly speaking. Silence conspicuous the. "To slowly return face enlarged his to kindly print distribution wide-spread this considering maybe to identify him important." Most of extremely bore work such this like also seeking chases useless much. At often happens nothing pertinent all.

"Above nicely walks she sexy much."

"But not again. Be quiet."

"No. Before explicitly instructed watchers garrulous all."

"Before not meant asshole sexist."

"Enough. Among usually allowed talk wide-ranging, the underneath freely associating accidents vital a lot of. But now distracts."

Benderson.

Silent all. Before easily approached the door wooden, his in front of clearly to recognize profile evident so. With then went Zemlinsky smiling theirs into. Definitely remembered expression smirking his, with always showed intimacy shared a before definitely fucked Zemlinsky sexy, the. Underneath clearly indicating March 31, mere a couple before initially kill days. Despairing. His before probably was involved death own the with brutally murdering Dehmel sliced the before deceitfully murdering suicide Sixto the. Following then was killed. Lowenthal frightened much?

Until suddenly strutted Schlaf, self-confident, that before always noticed ring obtrusive enough. Off quickly switched someone, prudent, the since previously playing disc. Unnoticed? No. "As far as diligently working, you incomparable. Yes. Notwithstanding, seriously warning, I, earnest, all inside forcefully advise you, reasonable, all to completely consider Lowenthal innocent. No near to inquisitively approaching him unconditional: each from away remain Lowenthal. Understood?" No. Concerning dubiously was timing questionable his.

III.

A little anxious, needed somehow to my disparate thoughts organize soundly. To that suspicious Lowenthal arrest immediately, against the captain's orders, would bring likely down some real trouble. To talk merely to the witness Lowenthal would bring also inside my superior's wrath. To ignore however, concerning all new evidence would rub unconscionably against my detective thinking. Hired likely behind, the rotten Benderson to kill brutally before his toned wife, to stage also following the false Sixto suiciding apparently. Concerning the foolish Benderson to kill then before the moron gardener to kill then following so surveillance discs would be seen never after so Benderson connection made never between. The primary cop investigating initially during the ubiquitous Benderson, changed radically into an unknown person killing ruthlessly underneath. The surveillance discs Fed-exed likely by the sexy secretary, to establish explicitly before a damning connection made unequivocally between the two killers.

To prove how?

Outside, an unanswered telephone rang continuously. Inside, many unanswered questions echoed equally. Below, the surveillance discs copied in case of any possible fingerprints to be extracted technologically. Above, the homicide team watched carefully still the copied discs to find hopefully in addition to some other evidence. Involve why during this policeman Benderson? To get paid? Possibly. Because of his Zemlinsky fucking? To murder? Implausibly. Before, the young Benderson lived ungenerously with his interested women, thinking how instead of all blessed them to be. Invariably. Concerning all of the interested women, gave never from the young Benderson, choosing instead of the indifferent Sultan to play. Greedily. From the broke beginning was always. For a lot of useful money could be certainly. Before, his bank records checked futilely. Outside, the unanswered telephone rang uninterruptedly near.

The pressing question: to proceed now, in spite of a few central uncertainties? To wait prudently, in addition to more concrete evidence gather irreproachably, in addition to the upstairs brass pissing not on? My alone decision to make. Insistently. Despite the captain's orders: go now. Underneath a nagging feeling mistaking badly because of my preoccupied desire to arrest against finally within the bastard Lowenthal. Believed honestly in my justified actions. Go. Now. Out.

CHAPTER 9

Fünf Klavierstücke
op. 23

V. Walzer

We knocked loudly. Gunshots four above. We heard definitely. Office upstairs from. We crashed quickly. Door resistant despite. It opened finally. Staircase recognized toward. Everyone moved quickly. Weapons conspicuous out. I flattened clumsily. Wall previewed against. Everyone ascended carefully. Hallway unknown inside. We gathered forebodingly. Door office around. Who murdered now? Lowenthal asshole by? It splintered suddenly. Office accessible into. We entered slowly. Light dim above. I scanned quickly. Room lavish about. It dominated saliently. Desk mahogany by. That dominated surprisingly. Lowenthal head upon. That dominated shockingly. Holes gaping throughout. Everything dominated visibly. Pool blood from. I heard quietly. Whispering rhythmic near. I focused difficultly. Darkness thick through. She standing stiffly. Weapon obvious beside. It touched threateningly. Temple Zemlinsky's against.

I blundered utterly. Wrong absolutely about. I required here. Attention undivided on. I would unavoidably. Re-examination regretful after. Everyone positioned expertly. Death Zemlinsky besides? We prevent how? Murders excessive because of. We quieted suddenly. Murmurs silent throughout. Nothing heard absolutely. Breathing inaudible among. We waited inexactly. Teleology lacking about. Everything suspended seemingly. Progress arrested within.

I wondered guiltily. Causes mistaken regarding. I desired primarily. Knowledge genuine because of. This murdering relentlessly. Motives undetected throughout. I desired truthfully. Role Benderson's in. His killing initially. Victim guilty between? I desired moreover. Culpability own in. I had desired greatly. Apprehension Lowenthal before. This deafened irrefutably. Others dead because of. All killing why? Suspicions existed but. I'd caused already. Fuck-up large by. My assuming prematurely. Patterns unheard beneath. I hadn't listened enough. Killer brutal as. I needed then. Zemlinsky alive in spite of. She to provide hopefully. Information missing throughout.

I looked down. Head Lowenthal upon. It shattered horrifically. Face destroyed beyond. She'd fired multiple. Rounds exploding into. She use earlier? Weapon Benderson on? This obliterating hysterically. Improvisation cadential within. This murdering viciously. Extemporaneity premeditated in addition to. Both combined schizophrenically. Cadenza rehearsed before. I had seen never. Head form without. It appeared indefinitely. Metaphors ineffectual about.

I bent closer. Mass liquescent near. I felt honestly. Nothing human except. Himself spilling uncontrollably. Revulsion public about. He lacked now. Discretion any regarding. Himself opened completely. Brain immodest exposed. Himself dripping slowly. Carpet once-grey onto. Those murdered always. Privacy lost from.

It was now. Action necessary before. Something happened else. Death more among. Everything stopped considerably. Gestures frozen since. Nothing moved perceptibly. Rhythm incomprehensible except. The expanding relentlessly. Pool red upon. That marked only. Time possible toward. What to do precisely? Zemlinsky alive for. Her to keep how? Charm threatening against? I stood slowly. Detective forceful despite. How to approach wisely? Murky room across. She immobilized stiffly. Arm akimbo apart from. I noticed now. Smith & Wesson same as. I considered briefly. Death secretarial in addition to. Nobody would blame definitely. Cop-killer dead despite. We'd bury somehow. Mouths shut against.

"You place slowly. Weapon your down." I spoke loudly. Silence shattered throughout. We rejoined fully. Time human throughout.

She remained rigidly. Statue still before. She thinking what? Head Lowenthal's opposite. She possessed certainly. Capacity violent beyond. This raging outwards. Different internal from. I tried again. "Zemlinsky calm throughout. We remain vigilantly. Zemlinsky armed against. We become unavoidably. Tension nervous against. You disarm now. Police relaxed because of. We'll talk calmly. Women two between."

She stood there. Smith and Wesson heavy against. She responsible least. Murders three at. She responsible possibly. Murders five for. I connected irrefutably. Diva slaughtering with. Myself looked critically. Detective fool upon. She remained motionlessly. Indifference larger against. I shrugged slightly.

"Choices three considering. You abate now. Weapon abandoned down. We talk sympathetically. One number among. You shoot suicidally. Death instantaneous as. We watch passively. Two number among. You try stupidly. Cop killer against. We shoot accurately. Zemlinsky dead before. We wounded never. Choice final among."

She sighed audibly. Officers edgy around. She shifted carefully. Arm left up. She transferred gently. Weapon other into. Herself crossed abruptly. Gesture Catholic despite. We tensed further. Point breaking next.

"I want now. Two only inside."

"Everyone leave quickly." Police gone from. She disarmed deliberately. Room quiet throughout. I holstered crisply. Head clear above. We stared finally. Faces alone across.

CHAPTER 10

Phantasy for Violin
with Piano Accompaniment
op. 47

"I was an artist, okay, since. And successfully I per-
formed absurd theater."

"Bravo regarding."

"So sarcastically. You want my story, yes? Before? Even
if disjointedly I speak, scattered killer, fuck, during, even if
distractedly."

I read her Miranda, yes, lest until forgetfully. "You nar-
rate all events, please, from wherever essentially they begin.
Simple task."

"Christ above. Because stereotypically you are deaf
cop. Fuck. Unless maybe you listen, limited detective, uh-
huh, near, carefully, I become dead suspect."

"Yeah? Against although truthfully I wouldn't object.
Less paperwork. Mazel tov."

"Except if solitarily, you remain ignorant detective.
Shit. For rather than silently, you need talkative killer, lady,

inside, so that eventually you understand." Long pause. "Damn. Regarding opposite furiously I killed. Stupid prick. Fuck. Into until uncontrollably I fired."

"Benderson weapon?"

"Yeah, before once. Pleasingly, it exploded, Lowenthal's head. Bang! Over and repeatedly. I continued. Good feeling."

"Really?"

"During while ecstatically. You understand? Real moment. Boo-Ya!"

"After? And now?"

"I lost my mind, detective, following after initially she was murdered. Dehmel. Fuck. Among, while typically we conspired, avaricious killers. Jesus. Considering, if greedily, I was irrational, lunatic. Uh-huh. Throughout, as long as, obviously, I loved bastard Lowenthal. Yes ma'am, plus, and, obviously, I loved Lowenthal's money, yes ma'am, besides, as much as. Identically. Everything was equal motivation, yeah. About, while, crazily I acted. Psycho bitch, yeah, despite while actually I knew better. Schizo. Hell above. And now, I talk."

"Sorry?"

"Regret? No. Concerning because remorsefully nothing done. Exhausted, bullets, alas, without and undeniably. This is a metaphor."

"Yes. As."

"Since still I am dangerous bitch, bitch. Opposite, although tiredly."

"You must be exhausted. "

"Yeah. Beyond. Although truthfully, this is unfinished performance, detective, about still crucially I have to tell my story, right, among, even though obviously everyone's dead. Successful detective, yeauh, above, since ultimately you caught the killer. "

"Uh-uh. Opposite. Because only you used up all victims. True that. Following in spite of stupidly I suspected bastard Lowenthal."

"Really?"

"Until when earlier we came Lowenthal's arrest. Chrissakes, by, although evidently everything misread moronic detective. So, above, in order that approximately I can understand this mess, really, concerning, because only your remains, necessary narrative. So, without unless, irrefutably I am lost."

"Lowenthal? Really? For since obviously he was partially guilty. Yes ma'am. Before because explicitly he approved our plan."

"Our?"

"Except that originally she would be missing person."

"She?"

"Beyond wherever eternally we'd hide her body. Adios. Without as much as completely we'd clam, proverbial peep. Right. Against because perversely I spoiled, disappearing plot. Shit. Against because ostentatiously I arranged wife's corpse. Fucking A. Beyond. And consequently more died. Pissed Lowenthal, la de dah, following, so that peevishly he washed his hands. Meh. Regarding. And then he wanted more money, oops, for in order to permanently his keep shut mouth."

"Huh?"

"For so that silently he could stay alive. Sixto."

"Jesus. To while uncomprehendingly I listen your story. Unbelievable! Amid as much as incidentally I catch a name. Maybe. Underneath I see possible glimmers, true, but even if, understandably this makes no sense."

"Detective, before whenever certainly I spoke crucial warning, detective, to in order that conceivably you might learn the truth, detective, despite even though incoherently, this is only way, detective, following wherever inadvertently I might lead. True story. Detective, for in order that no this to tell other way. Yes. Inside as long as attentively you listen vital facts, detective, from as much as likely they will emerge, no doubt. Okay? Following since stupidly, I staged wife's murder, bravo, since that greedily he demanded more, Sixto, detective, to although initially he was given five grand, detective, concerning for."

"Why?"

"He saw love-struck Benderson, detective, with and repeatedly me flirting."

"Killer Benderson?"

"Yep. For while lovingly he would do necessary anything. Mother of God. For provided that possibly I'd fuck, obliging Benderson. Alas. About and also he killed blackmailing Sixto. And about that modestly I arranged fake suicide. Okay. Inside after alone he shot, *vivant tableau*. *Voilà*. Along in order that cleverly we implicated idiotic gardener. Ew. Concerning as long as continuously I hated, stupid fuck. Dipshit. Behind whenever always he'd check my ass. Oo la la. Regarding because happily I poisoned the motherfucker. Yeauh. With since sneakily I drugged some propofol. Shoot shoot. Up after tightly I tied his hands. Uh-huh. Into and then I drove postal driveway, mmm, across so conspicuously everyone would see stupid prick. D'oh. Off when almost I removed his clothes, damn, but as though already I did Benderson's body, okay, against, and artistically I hate all repetition, boring! during. Even if suggestively. You need tape recorder, detective?"

"Outside, in order that accurately, they're recording your statement."

"Huh? Before, although legally, you never asked. My rights, detective, about in case possibly I change my mind. You think? Despite lest, troublesomely I plead not guilty. Detective, besides by the time now I don't remember that question, you know, without, as long as, honestly I started talking any warning."

"No. On as long as certainly my was recorded Miranda reading."

"Really? By although even recording can lie, tricky police. Detective, following whenever, maybe I take a hostage, yeah, with so spectacularly I escape Detective Fruscella?"

"No."

"Outside while certainly you are cocky motherfucker, detective. Inside? Even if threateningly I take my gun? Huh? Considering although? Only I am joking. Slapstick, right? Despite how, generously I realize vital narration, detective, but after, honestly, I've got no plans. No. Until nor after. I do remember your Miranda, detective, regarding since. Where I was? Gardener's murder, oh yeah. Into in order that easily I placed exhaust hose. Hee hee. Near and surreptitiously I watched his face, detective, as once stupidly he awakened, anxious eyes, detective, beyond even though, indescribably they looked. Ignorant terror. Yeah. For as long as awhile, they wondered, questioning lungs, damn, regarding and why they were failing. Air. Christ above. Until finally he understood. Beautiful enlightenment. Ooo. Unlike."

"For truthfully whom?"

"Asking excellent question detective. For both definitely. I'm no sadist, God, but once, unforgettably that was some sight. Sweet Jesus. Beyond and satisfyingly, I admit, gardener's killing, ouch, plus, in order that clearly I to warn dangerous Lowenthal, bastard, for until patiently him to send absolutely nothing, fool, with since just him to wait, no communication, detective, from as long as necessarily."

"He ignored your message."

"Yeah. Following as much as understandably he got spooked. Coward. Detective, before, because truly you think killer Lowenthal?"

"Yeah. Before."

"Because?"

"Statistically many kill their wives, right? Against unless otherwise, that's our default motive."

"That's it?"

"Besides, since undeniably victims connected common boss, right?"

"Plus because clearly he's a man. Yes?"

"Regarding as rarely we kill multiple victims, you bet."

"During so ironically you underestimated this narrator."

"Okay. Beyond that, why you did kill detective Benderson?"

"Whoa. Against since abruptly you change the subject, detective, underneath as if seemingly I hit a nerve? Okay. With once personally he was pretty important, right? Between after initially he loved this secretary. Yes, despite while stereotypically I did not return cop love, yeah, for as long as noirishly I manipulated said lover, detective, for as much as lovingly he would do absolutely anything. Okay. Until but eventually he discovered Lowenthal love, duh, excluding, so uncompromisingly he gave rigorous ultimatum. Well, against that necessarily I resisted. No choice, detective. Despite so previously, he turned dangerous liability, detective, into by the time. Regrettably, I had to shoot valuable Benderson, detective."

"Into so why he placed polished dumpster?"

"Ah, off in order to deceitfully you throw the scent, detective, by while seemingly he killed mobster Hemple. Ta da."

"Like so why he scrubbed savior Jesus?"

"Damn. Concerning whenever aesthetically, I overstate. Blatant baroque. Fuck. Besides since glaringly I used cop-killer bullets. Hmm. About and definitely, I admit, *de trop*. Control, detective, regarding as long as, always, my has been major flaw."

"Christ."

"Regarding, only if artistically. I meant no disrespect, detective. Unlike after horticulturally, this was self defense, yeah, since unless rapidly I abandoned Lowenthal plans, damn, to in case immediately he would go the FBI. Motherfuckers. Concerning if successfully, my would be threatened life. Look, during in case, seriously…"

"You killed a cop."

"Fuck! Regarding, than ethically he is more important? Really? Before because romantically you shared lukewarm bed? No? Since because officially he was police detective? Fuck. Underneath although spectacularly he was brutal thug. Detective, concerning so poorly you listen. The end. Concerning, for finally I can't give your desire, detective." Following but now nothing audible strange silence. Hmm. Through even though, loudly,

"I need something else. Damn. Amid. Because…"

"Really, there's nothing else, detective. Inside or externally."

"There has to be. Colossal waste, fuck, against if not."

"What will be my sentence?"

NOTE TO READERS

This writing was based on the attempt to translate musical ideas from the work of Arnold Schoenberg. In the more serial pieces, where he used tones, I used parts of speech. *Stretti*, inversions and other techniques were sometime employed. In the "atonal" *Erwartung* chapter, I was struck by the happy coincidence that the librettist for the *monodram* might have been related to Freud's Anna O.

Problems remain.